For Paul
C.F.

For Joseph Thompson with love
K.S.

Copyright © 2006 by Good Books, Intercourse, PA 17534
International Standard Book Number:
ISBN-13: 978-1-56148-547-5;
ISBN-10: 1-56148-547-0
Library of Congress Catalog Card Number: 2006004466

Text copyright © Claire Freedman, 2006
Illustrations copyright © Kristina Stephenson 2006

Original edition published in Great Britain in 2006 by Gullane Children's Books, an imprint of Pinwheel Limited, Winchester House, 259-269 Old Marylebone Road, London, NW1 5XJ, England.

Printed and bound in China

Library of Congress Cataloging-in-Publication Data:
Freedman, Claire.
New kid in town / Claire Freedman ; [illustrated by] Kristina Stephenson.
p. cm.
Summary: When Mouse arrives in town, the other residents are quick to welcome him but also to warn about the Big Wolf, whose size, green teeth, and snapping jaws are terrible to behold.
ISBN-13: 978-1-56148-547-5 (hardcover)
[1. Mice--Fiction. 2. Wolves--Fiction. 3. Prejudices--Fiction. 4. Animals--Fiction.] I. Stephenson, Kristina, ill. II. Title.
PZ7.F87275New 2006
[E]--dc22
2006004466

New Kid In Town

Claire Freedman

Kristina Stephenson

Intercourse, PA 17534
800/762-7171
www.GoodBks.com

Mouse was the New Kid In Town. He bounced in from over the hill, looking for a new place to live, and came upon Badger's Bakery. "Hello!" said Mouse, strolling in. "I'm the New Kid In Town."

"Welcome!" Badger replied. "You'll love living in our town. It's the best place for apricot muffins." "But," Badger added, "watch out for the nasty Big Wolf who lives on the hill. He's huge and hairy, and wild and scary. **BEWARE!**"

Mouse bought some apricot muffins to eat in the park. Giraffe came and sat next to him. "Hello," said Giraffe. "So you're the New Kid In Town?" "Yes!" said Mouse.

"This is a very friendly place," said Giraffe. "But," she whispered, "**BEWARE** of the horrible Big Wolf who lives on the hill. He's ugly and mean, and his teeth are slime green. Watch out!"

That afternoon, Mouse was admiring a very pretty, empty cottage when Donkey came along.

"You must be the New Kid In Town," said Donkey.

"That's me!" said Mouse.

"Have you visited our skating rink yet?" asked Donkey. "We have competitions with exciting prizes."

"I love skating!" cried Mouse.
"Come along, then," whispered Donkey.
"But keep an eye out for the horrible Big Wolf.
His jaws go **KER-RUNCH**, and he'll
eat you for lunch. Take care!"

The following morning, Mouse moved
his belongings into the pretty cottage.
He swept and dusted, unpacked and tidied.
Soon everything was spick and span.

Mouse folded up his apron.
"Perfect!" he smiled. "Just
one thing needs sorting out."

Mouse marched out, past Badger's Bakery, through
the park, alongside the skating rink, and up the hill . . .
the hill where Big Wolf lived.
"I'm not scared of the Big Bad Wolf," he sang.
Mouse had only taken a few more steps when . . .

"Grrrrrrgh!"

He heard
a horrible,
horrible noise!
And, suddenly,
out sprang . . .

Big
Wolf!

"Who are you?" snarled Big Wolf.
"I'm the New Kid In Town!" said Mouse.
"Perhaps you haven't heard about me yet," Big Wolf sneered.
"I'm big and I'm hairy! I'm wild and I'm scary!"

"I think you look rather smart and neat," smiled Mouse. "What a nice thing to say," replied Big Wolf shyly. "No one's ever paid me a compliment before!"

Then, suddenly, Big Wolf frowned.
"You think I'm ugly and mean, because my
teeth are slime green – don't you?" Big Wolf growled.
Mouse shook his head. "Ugly? Not with that cheerful smile,"
he said. "I'm sure you're not mean either."

"I'm not!" said Big Wolf, really smiling now.
"And my teeth are only green from chewing grass."
"I could lend you a toothbrush," Mouse offered.
"So kind!" said Big Wolf.

"But my big jaws go *KER-RUNCH*.
Aren't you scared I'll eat
you for lunch?!"
"You wouldn't eat me,"
Mouse replied, "now that
we've become such
good friends!"

"Whaaaah! Whaaaaaah!"

Big Wolf sobbed loudly on Mouse's shoulder. "I've never had a friend before!" he howled. "There, there," said Mouse. "Blow your nose on this. Then come back to town with me."

"But I can't come to town with you," said Wolf.
"Why not?" asked Mouse.
"Because . . . I'm scared," sniffed Big Wolf.
"They all hate me down there!"
"Bye, then," waved Mouse.

At the bottom of the hill, Mouse could see
Badger, Giraffe and Donkey waiting anxiously.
"Yooo-Hooo!" waved Mouse cheerily.
"Come and meet Big Wolf. He'd like
to come and live with us all!"
"Not likely!" said Badger.
"You're joking!" gasped Donkey.
"Help!" cried Giraffe.

"See?" said Big Wolf. "No one wants me!"
He burst into a flood of tears again.
"Don't worry," Mouse told him. "I'll soon sort this out."

"Come on, everyone," Mouse said.
"Big Wolf may look wild and scary,
but it's not his fault he's hairy.
And although his eyes are yellow,
he's a friendly kind of fellow!"

"Hmm," said Badger, "I suppose he's never really done anyone any harm."
"That's true," said Giraffe and Donkey. "Maybe we could give him a chance."

Suddenly Big Wolf's tummy rumbled very loudly.
"Oh dear, I don't like the sound of that!" said Donkey in a scared voice.
"N e i t h e r   d o   w e . . . ," trembled the others.

"GGGRRR!"

"I'm **STARVING!**" Big Wolf said.
"I could just fancy a tasty . . ."

". . . BAKED BADGER?" gulped Badger.

". . . GRILLED GIRAFFE?"
gasped Giraffe.

". . . B-B-BUTTERED
DONKEY?" stuttered Donkey.

"Surely not . . .
MOUSE MOUSSE?" giggled Mouse.

"Yuck, and Double YUCK!" laughed Big Wolf.
"I was thinking of apricot muffins."
"HOORAY!" chorused Badger,
Giraffe, Donkey and Mouse.
"Apricot muffins it is then –
as many as you like!

"After all, you are
going to be the ...

NEW KID IN TOWN!"